SPY VS. SPY

ADAPTED BY KATE HOWARD

SCHOLASTIC INC.

ISBN 978-0-545-82553-5

10 9 8 7 6 5 4 3 2   15 16 17 18 19

Printed in the U.S.A.   40
First printing 2015

A SECRET MISSION

"Things are looking up," Cole said. He and the other ninja were on Master Chen's island for the Tournament of Elements. They had come to find their friend Zane, who was a prisoner. When Cole lost his tournament battle, he became Chen's prisoner, too.

"We came here to find a friend," Cole told Karlof, another elemental fighter. "I found him. All I gotta do is get Zane and get outta here!"

"But it's impossible to escape this place," said Karlof. The two new friends were stuck working in Master Chen's fortune cookie factory.

Cole shrugged. "I'm working out the details. But first, I gotta let the other ninja know I'm bustin' Zane out." He held up a tiny slip of paper.

"You put a message in a cookie?" Karlof gasped. "I hope you have the good fortune for it to end up in the right hands."

Upstairs in the palace, Master Chen was hosting a banquet. "Let's celebrate the eight contestants who made it to the second round!" he cheered.

But the ninja didn't trust Master Chen. They knew he was trying to steal everyone's powers. Jay, Kai, and Lloyd had formed a secret alliance with the other Elemental Masters—everyone but Shade, Master of Shadow.

"If you plan to stop Chen," Garmadon told the ninja, "you'll need everyone on board."

Clouse leaned toward Chen. "Our guests have allied themselves."

"Do they know about the spell?" Chen hissed.

Clouse shook his head. "Not yet."

Chen stood up. "I know there are rumors that I am stealing everyone's powers . . . I am," he announced.

Everyone gasped.

"But it's all for this staff!" Chen continued.

"The staff holds the powers of your fallen foes," Chen said. "The last person standing in my tournament will win it!"

"What about the spell?" Lloyd asked.

"Spell? What spell?" Clouse asked.

"Don't believe him," Lloyd told the others. "It's a trick!"

"Why should we believe you, Lloyd?" asked Shade.

Clouse chuckled. "The alliance is crumbling. Very clever, Master."

"We need to find that spell," Jay whispered. He turned to a Kabuki dancer who kept whacking him with her fan. "Cut it out!"

"Jay, it's me—Nya," the dancer whispered. "I'm undercover."

Kai grinned. "Then you can get close to Clouse's spell book!"

Nya nodded. "I'll look into it. But you need to look into something, too. *You* have a spy!"

Skylor, Master of Amber, cracked open her fortune cookie. "Look! Cole and Zane are breaking out. You're lucky this message didn't end up in the wrong hands."

"Cole found Zane! I can't believe it," Kai cried. "Thanks, Skylor. It's good to know there are some people here we can trust."

"Who do you think the spy is?" Jay asked.

Lloyd stared at Shade. "I have my suspicions."

Nya hurried away to call Dareth, who'd helped her sneak on to the island. "Dareth, are you there?"

The Brown Ninja answered from Nya's hidden mobile unit. "Loud and proud, Nya. Talk to me."

"I'm going to find the spell while the ninja sniff out a spy," Nya told him.

"Aye aye, Samurai X," agreed Dareth. "Brown Ninja out."

THE ESCAPE PLAN

Back at the factory, Cole was working on his escape plan. He needed to steal the guards' keys. He distracted them by grabbing some noodles.

"Don't touch the merchandise!" a guard hollered. "Get him!"

"Let there be food!" Cole cried, gobbling a handful of cookies. "Now I'm runnin' on cookie power!"

Cole used a long string of noodles to swing himself over the guards. "Woo-hoo!"

Splat! The noodle rope broke, and Cole fell on top of a guard.

"Got you!" shouted the guard. Cole burped in his face.

The guard dragged Cole through the factory and threw him into a jail cell.

Cole grinned. "It was all worth it"—he lifted the guard's keys into the air—"for these!"

"Cole?" murmured Zane. Cole was leaning over his friend, unlocking his chains. "You have returned."

Cole smiled. "Of course. I made a promise. Now, c'mere, you shiny, new tin can." He hugged his friend. "Can you feel the love?"

"No," Zane said honestly. "But the longer we stand here, the less time we have to escape."

"You were always the smart one," Cole said. "Let's go!"

Meanwhile, Nya had sneaked into Chen's study and was examining the Book of Spells. "Page 102 . . . 122 . . . 149. This changes everything!"

Nya tore the page out of the book. Then she heard footsteps.

Outside in the hallway, a guard said, "There's been a breach in the factory. Master Cole has gone missing."

Clouse cackled. "Release my pet. She'll make sure he doesn't escape."

Down in the tunnels, Zane and Cole were lost. "Not that way. That will only take us back to where we started," said Zane.

Suddenly, there was a rattling sound.

"We need to move!" shouted Cole. "Trust me, you'll want to keep up."

Zane swung his head around and met Clouse's pet—an enormous serpent!

Zane and Cole ran as fast as they could. But they kept bumping into the serpent's scaly body.

"Another dead end," said Cole.

"The serpent's strategy appears to be to surround us and coil inward," noted Zane. "Very clever."

"Yeah, well, my strategy is not to be eaten!" cried Cole.

"Pixal: Calculate escape scenarios," Zane said. Pixal was a Nindroid whose hard drive was hidden inside Zane's head.

"Calculating escape routes. Activating explosives," she replied.

"Pixal?" Cole said. "You've got a *girl* stuck in your head?"

Zane tossed a handful of explosives in a circle, creating a hole for him and Cole to fall through. *Boom!*

"I'm gonna like the new you," Cole said.

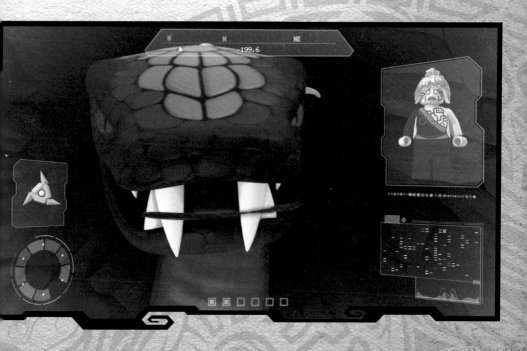

SPY GAMES

Upstairs, Jay, Kai, and Lloyd were meeting with the Elemental Masters. "No one leaves this room until we find out who's passing information to Chen," said Lloyd.

Neuro began reading minds. "Someone here isn't who they say they are."

Skylor cut in. "Maybe I should use your power and see inside your head."

"This is what Chen wants!" Kai said. "For us to fight. There has to be a better way."

Garmadon nodded. "There is. Everyone who's ever worked for Chen has an Anacondrai tattoo on their back. Find the tattoo, find the spy."

Neuro stepped forward to show everyone his back was bare.

"Who's next?" asked Lloyd.

Back in the banquet hall, Chen was enjoying a Kabuki performance. Nya slipped into the room. She hid the spell page inside her kimono. Then she tried to fit in with the other dancers.

"Tell me they've caught the escaped prisoner," Chen growled at Clouse.

"Not yet," Clouse said. "But I have far worse news: Someone has stolen the spell!"

"Do you need the page to do the spell?" Chen asked.

Clouse shook his head. "No. But if the ninja find it, the fighters will know we've lied."

"Then we must find that page!" Chen cried.

Clouse looked at the spell book. There was a white smudge on the cover—Kabuki makeup! "We have a spy! Guards, search every servant in this room!"

THE SPY HUNT

Loud music interrupted the search for the spy. Dareth had accidentally flipped a switch, and now his favorite rock music was blasting all over the island.

"That sound is coming from the spy," said Chen. "Find the signal, find the spy!"

"You heard him: Search the island!" Clouse ordered. He turned to Nya and the other Kabuki. "As for you . . . stay put."

The ninja were still seeking the spy in their midst.

"Only two left," said Lloyd, looking at Skylor and Shade.

"I hate to do this," Kai said to Skylor. "But can I see your back, please?"

"Wait!" Lloyd interrupted. "Where did Shade go?"

"He's disappearing through his own shadow!" said Jay.

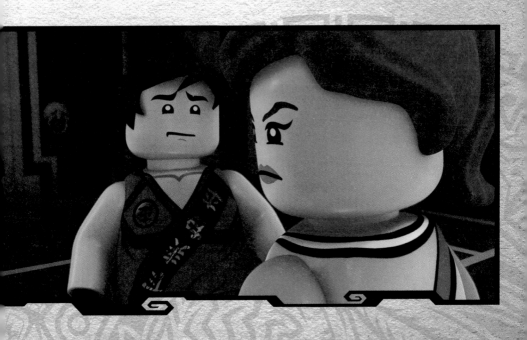

"I ain't your spy, and I ain't your friend, either. That staff will be mine!" Shade hissed.

Everyone scrambled to catch Shade. But he dodged them all and disappeared.

Kai turned to Skylor. "Sorry I didn't trust you."

"If you still think I'm the spy, watch me walk out that door," Skylor replied. As she strode out, Kai could see there was no tattoo on her back.

In the banquet hall, Chen sighed happily.
"Kabuki are always pleased to serve me."

Nya fanned Chen and pretended she was
happy to serve. She had to, or Chen would
know *she* was the spy.

"Have you found where the signal's coming
from?" Chen asked Clouse.

"We haven't found anything on the island
yet," said Clouse. "But we will."

Nya slipped away from Chen and called Dareth. "Dareth! They're coming! Do you read me? They're coming for you!"

Dareth looked out the mobile unit's window. "*Ahh!* Where's the cloak button?" He pressed a few buttons, but it was too late. The guards were almost on him.

Dareth revved the motor. "Now, let's test what's under this hood!"

The guards dove out of the way as Dareth blasted toward them. Blade chariots and copters began chasing him.

Trouble was, Dareth had no idea how to drive his getaway car. "Somebody get me outta here!" he screamed.

On command, a mini-robot popped up and took over the steering wheel. "Autopilot: initiated."

"Score one for the Brown Ninja!" Dareth whooped as he took down a blade chariot. Then he realized the mini-robot was driving them toward a cliff. "Bad autopilot! Bad!"

Dareth slammed on the brakes, and the mobile unit skidded onto its side. There was no escape—he was surrounded.

"Nya, I've been taken hostage! You're on your own."

Back in Chen's lair, Nya's comm unit lit up. Chen could hear everything Dareth was saying!

"So *you're* the spy," Chen said, grabbing her. "The spell!"

Nya wiggled away from him. "By the way, your feet stink!"

Chen grabbed his staff and shot ice at her. But Nya was too fast.

"Get her. And get that spell!" Chen shouted.

Down in the tunnels, Zane and Cole hid as two guards passed. "We have to find the spy. Forget about the escaped factory worker; Chen will make the other workers pay," one guard told the other.

"I have to go back," Cole whispered. "A ninja protects those who cannot protect themselves."

Zane nodded. "And a ninja never leaves another ninja's side."

Cole smiled. "We'll get off this island, Zane. But it's either all of us or none of us."

Outside the palace, Nya kept running as Clouse and the guards chased her.

Clouse grabbed for her, but Nya kicked him away. Then she raced up a rooftop and found cover in the forest below. She was gone!

"Find her!" Clouse screamed to the guards.

A guard hurried into Chen's throne room.

"My spy, have they found the girl?" Chen asked.

"No," said the guard. "But you have a bigger problem." The guard began to change shape. It was Skylor! "Cole's got the Ninja of Ice, Father."

Chen smiled. "Thank you, daughter. The Master of Form's power has proved useful to you. The ninja's time here is done. Tomorrow, we will break up the ninja . . . forever!"